Singing Away the Dark

This story is dedicated to my mother, Dina Woodward, and to the memory
of our good neighbour, Marjorie Miller Neudorf. — xoxo love Caro

To my father and his long winter walks to school. — Julie

Special edition published in 2017 by Simply Read Books. First published in 2010. www.simplyreadbooks.com Text © 2010 Caroline Woodward Illustrations © 2010 Julie Morstad. All rights reserved. No part of this publication may be reproduced, stored in a retrieval system, or transmitted, in any form or by any means, electronic, mechanical, photocopying, recording or otherwise, without the written permission of the publisher. The publisher does not have any control over and does not assume any responsibility for author or third-party websites or their content. We gratefully acknowledge for their financial support of our publishing program the Canada Council for the Arts, the BC Arts Council, and the Government of Canada through the Canada Book Fund. Special edition book design by Heather Lohnes. Original book design by Elisa Gutiérrez. Printed in Korea.   10 9 8 7 6 5 4 3 2 1

Library and Archives Canada
Cataloguing in Publication

Woodward, Caroline, 1952-, author
    Singing away the dark / Caroline Woodward ;
illustrations by Julie Morstad. -- Special edition.
ISBN 978-1-77229-019-6 (hardback)
    I. Morstad, Julie, illustrator II. Title.
PS8595.O657S56 2016   j813'.54   C2016-903440-2

Caroline Woodward

Singing Away the Dark

illustrations by Julie Morstad

SIMPLY READ BOOKS

When I was six and went to school,
I walked a long, long way...

I leave my house, so nice and warm,
on a windy winter's day.

I walk alone down our long hill.
Then home is out of sight.

I take a breath and stand up tall
and grip my lunch pail tight.

"I must be brave," I tell myself.
"The school bus will not wait..."

I squeeze between the wires.
I have no time for gates.

I don't allow myself to stop
to look between the trees,
to peer at shapes that shift and hide
where it's too dark to see.

But creaks and groans and hoots and howls
still creep into my ears.

I take a breath...

and *sing* until...

the darkness disappears.

The cattle block the road ahead.
The bull is munching hay.

I softly sing to calm myself
and plan the safest way.

I see a line of big, old trees,
marching up the hill.
"I salute you, Silent Soldiers.
Help me if you will."

"Silent Soldiers, please protect me.
Stand beside me, tall and strong.
Help me cross this Wild Beast Valley,"
I sing my army on.

Now onward past Ms. Margie's house.
I hurry on my way.
"Have fun at school," she calls to me.
And I sing back, "Okay!"

The winds come howling from the North.
My eyes begin to sting.
I struggle on through endless snow,
and all the time I sing.

I sing for sun, I sing for strength,

I sing for warm toes, too.

*I am so happy when I see
two headlights blaze in view.*

*I climb on board to warmth and smiles
to start a new school day...*

When I was six and walked a mile
and sang the dark away.

Caroline Woodward grew up on a Cecil Lake homestead in B.C.'s Peace River region, where all the children are brave and tough and where she really did walk a mile to her school bus stop, uphill both ways. She lives on the Lennard Island Lightstation at the entrance to Clayoquot Sound, near Tofino, Canada. Find out more about Caroline and her books at www.carolinewoodward.ca.

Julie Morstad is an author and illustrator who makes drawings for books and many other things. She lives in Vancouver, Canada, with her husband and three kids, who all like to draw every day, too.